WORKING HARD WITH THE MIGHTY TRACTOR TRAILER AND BULLDOZER™

Written by Justine Korman
Illustrated by Steven James Petruccio

SCHOLASTIC INC.
New York   Toronto   London   Auckland   Sydney

Look for these other books about Tonka trucks:

Working Hard with the Busy Fire Truck

Working Hard with the Mighty Dump Truck

Working Hard with the Mighty Loader

Working Hard with the Mighty Mixer

Building the New School

Fire Truck to the Rescue

Working Hard with the Rescue Helicopter

Big City Dump Truck

Big Farm Tractor

ISBN 0-590-13450-7

13 14 15 16 17 18 19 20

Printed in the U.S.A.   23

First printing, May 1997

Sam is a truck driver. The only person who loves trucks more than Sam is his son, Logan.

On this spring morning, Sam says good-bye to Logan.
It is time to go to work!

Sam drives his pickup truck on the highway. There isn't much traffic this early in the morning.

There are delivery vans bringing goods to local stores. A big 18-wheel semi is on the road. Sam used to drive a big rig. He would drive all the way across the country and sleep in the cab of his truck. But now Sam likes to work closer to home.

Soon Sam arrives at the Tuff Trucks Trucking Company.
The company has all kinds of construction trucks. Many
of the trucks are called earthmovers because they are
used to move dirt and rocks so people can build houses,
stores, schools, roads, and more!

Sam goes to the dispatcher to find out where he will be working today. The dispatcher's job is to tell each driver where to go and how to get there.

Today, Sam and his bulldozer are going to level the foundation for a new home. The bulldozer is an "off-road" truck. It can't ride on the highway because it is too slow.

Off-road trucks have special tires for working on loose
or muddy ground. Bulldozers have crawler tracks that
spread their weight over a larger area than regular tires.
That's why bulldozers don't sink in the mud, even
though they are very heavy.

Some bulldozers weigh over 10 tons! Some are much smaller. Little bulldozers are sometimes called calfdozers, just as baby bulls are called calfs.

Sam will use another truck to take the bulldozer to the construction site. This truck is called a tractor trailer. It is a two-piece truck. The tractor holds the engine that pulls the trailer. Some tractors are strong enough to pull two trailers! They can drop one trailer in one town and drive straight on to the next town.

Sam drives his tractor trailer from the parking lot to the Tuff Trucks garage. The company mechanic will check Sam's truck. Trucks are valuable equipment. The Tuff Trucks Company keeps their trucks in top form.

Sam's tractor has a tilt-forward cab. This makes it easier for the mechanic to check the engine.

The mechanic also checks the coupling unit that connects the tractor to the trailer. The coupling unit swivels so the tractor part of the truck can turn around a corner before the trailer does.

A young mechanic pumps fuel into Sam's truck. Most cars run on gasoline. But most trucks use a heavier, cheaper fuel called diesel.

Now Sam is ready to drive his bulldozer up the ramp onto the back of his tractor trailer. It's time to hit the road!

First, Sam drives on a highway. Then he turns onto a smaller road.

Finally, Sam arrives at the construction site. It doesn't look like much yet. But soon this will be a family's home.

So far the workers have chopped down several trees. A logging truck will carry the tree trunks to a paper mill. A dump truck will haul away the branches and brush.

Now it is time for the bulldozer to do its job.
Dozing means pushing dirt and rocks out of
the way. Bulldozers use strong steel blades to
make the ground level enough for building.

Sam angles the blade to control where the soil will be pushed. He can raise and lower the blade, or tilt it forward and backward. Driving a bulldozer takes a lot of skill.

Sam must break up this little hill — or the new house will be crooked!

A loader puts the extra dirt into a dump truck. The dump truck will carry the dirt to a lower spot where the homeowners want to plant a garden.

The bulldozer's exhaust pipe doesn't point down like a car's pipe does. It points up to avoid the flying mud and rocks that are always around a busy bulldozer.

That is why Sam and the other workers all wear hard hats.
Building things can be dangerous!

After lunch, Sam finishes leveling the ground. Now workers use wooden pegs and strings to mark where the walls of the house will be. Soon they will pour concrete for the foundation.

Sam wonders who will live in this house. Will there be a young child who loves trucks like Logan does?

Sam is happy to get home. Now he can play with
Logan — and Logan's toy trucks!